Little Pup Goes Down the Road

by Robin Edward
illustrated by Richard Hoit

Harcourt
SCHOOL PUBLISHERS

ISBN 10: 0-15-350629-6
ISBN 13: 978-0-15-350629-1

Ordering Options
ISBN 10: 0-15-350598-2 (Grade 1 On-Level Collection)
ISBN 13: 978-0-15-350598-0 (Grade 1 On-Level Collection)
ISBN 10: 0-15-357788-6 (package of 5)
ISBN 13: 978-0-15-357788-8 (package of 5)

2 3 4 5 6 7 8 9 10 179 15 14 13 12 11 10 09 08 07

Little Pup gave a big sigh. "I am tired of this yard," he said. "I want to see what the rest of the earth is like." He dug under the wall by the table.

2

He put a branch down to hide
where he had dug. He thought he was
fooling his mother. Then, out he went.
He did not know that his mother was
following him.

"The earth is very big!" cried Little Pup. "There is so much to see!" Down the road he went.

He chased a cat. It climbed high up in a tree. He peeked here. He sniffed there.

Little Pup played in some leaves.
It was so much fun! He forgot it would
be night soon.

Then he looked around him, and
his eyes opened wide. There were
lots of dark shapes under the light of
the stars. He wished he was at home,
safe in his yard.

All of a sudden, Little Pup saw
a dark shape coming closer. What
could it be? The shape got bigger
as it came closer.

Then Little Pup saw that it was his mother! "You are not all alone," said Mother. "I was following you! You must never go out of the yard on your own."

"Yes," said Little Pup. "The earth is too big for little me." Then Little Pup and his mother went home.